Atlas Adventure

Written and illustrated by Nadine Cowan

Collins

Chapter 1

Olivia skated up to the window of Blue Mahoes restaurant and pressed her face against the warm glass. It was the summer holidays and her best friend Aniyah and Aniyah's cousin EJ were helping at their family restaurant.

As Olivia pulled the door open, the smell of fried fish and creamed coconut wafted towards her.

Olivia noticed white dust in Aniyah's hair. "What's that?"

Aniyah glared at EJ. "It's flour. We were helping Cook make fried dumplings and EJ started a flour fight. Aunty Pam told us off. She said our great grandma came to England from Jamaica on a ship, started the business in her living room and worked hard to get this restaurant, so we should be more respectful."

"You covered my trainers with flour," EJ said, "so we're even. Come on, let's play!"

3

On the table was the Ludi board, which usually hung on the wall of the restaurant. It was a large wooden board with four brightly coloured squares in each corner and a border of smaller squares. In the centre of the board was the home square, which had painted masks on each side. An inscription on the board read:

Roll double six, or double three,
let's learn about your history.

4

Olivia loved playing the game with her friends. Something amazing happened every time! EJ threw the dice and moved his counter five spaces.

Aniyah threw next. One dice hit the board and landed on a six. The other landed on its edge and flipped over. It was a six!

Before Aniyah could pick up her counter, the board began to pulse and flicker like a firefly. The table trembled and bursts of light flashed from the board. The colours danced in the whites of the children's eyes before a tornado formed, spun into a wormhole, and pulled them in.

Chapter 2

Aniyah felt the sun's hot rays and smelt sea salt in the air. When she opened her eyes, she found herself standing in a large crowd of smartly dressed people. Most of them had suitcases. Some were laughing and smiling, but others looked sad.

"I'm going to have tea with the king and queen," said a voice in the crowd.

"Dry your eyes; your mother will be waiting on the other side," said another.

Aniyah was wearing clothes she didn't recognise: a blouse, skirt, knee-length socks and Mary Jane shoes.

Olivia was wearing the same clothes as Aniyah. Beads of sweat were forming on her face. EJ was wearing an oversized suit and shiny leather shoes.

"Where are we?" Olivia asked.

"An island?" Aniyah pointed to the palm trees in the distance.

"Everyone sounds just like Aunty Pam," said EJ.

He reached into his pocket and pulled out a small leather-bound book.

5001001

BRITISH PASSPORT

JAMAICA

MR ELIJAH BROWN

"It's a passport!" Olivia said. "Are we in Jamaica?"

A thin piece of paper was poking out of the passport.

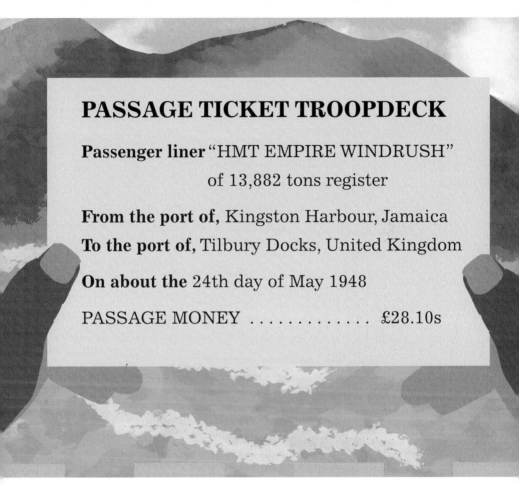

PASSAGE TICKET TROOPDECK

Passenger liner "HMT EMPIRE WINDRUSH"
of 13,882 tons register

From the port of, Kingston Harbour, Jamaica
To the port of, Tilbury Docks, United Kingdom

On about the 24th day of May 1948

PASSAGE MONEY £28.10s

It was a ticket. When Olivia and Aniyah felt in
their pockets, they had passports and tickets too.

"We've gone back in time to 1948!"

A foghorn sounded in the distance.

"Let's follow everyone else," Aniyah said.

As they followed the crowd, a huge ship with the words *Empire Windrush London* came into view. EJ's face lit up. "Wow! We're going on a ship!"

Olivia, EJ and Aniyah's excitement grew as they stepped onto the gangplank. Onboard, they felt the bobbing of the ship's hull bathing in the ebb and flow of the sea as though it was bopping to the calypso music being played on the ship. They heard a passenger say the ship had already been to Trinidad.

A man was checking people's tickets. EJ showed him his.

"You're on the troop deck with the boys and men. Join that group over there."

EJ looked at Aniyah and Olivia. A ship adventure sounded exciting at first but bunking on his own wasn't his idea of fun. He waved at Olivia and Aniyah and followed his group.

Chapter 3

EJ hoped that inside the ship would be cooler than outside, but it got hotter and hotter. He was handed a heavy blanket, but he wished it was an ice-cold drink. As soon as they arrived on the troop deck, EJ took off his jacket.

"Where we're going, you'll be needing that soon enough."

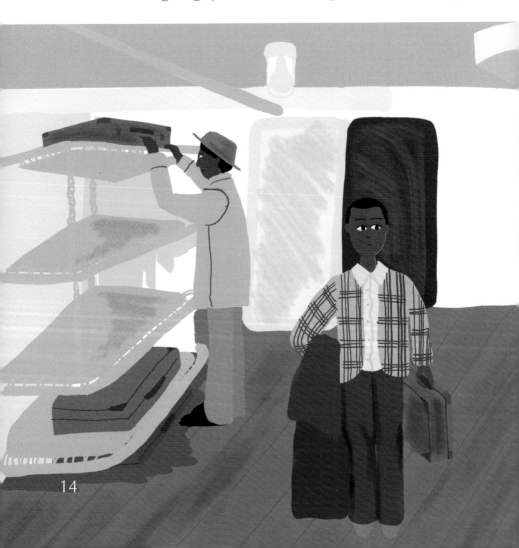

EJ looked back and saw a young man grinning at him.

"I'm Sam King," he said. "I joined the Royal Air Force as an engineer in the Second World War and was stationed in England. Believe me, it's colder there than bathing in a snow cone."

"Why are you going back?" asked EJ.

"When the war was over, I had to return to Jamaica, but I didn't want to work on my father's farm," Sam explained.

Another man drew near to Sam and EJ. "The hurricane destroyed the cane and banana fields. Things have been hard since," he said. "What's it like in England? I heard there's lots of jobs, and the streets are paved with gold."

"A lot of the buildings in London were damaged in the war," Sam replied, "but hopefully there will be plenty of jobs. Don't look so worried, it will be all right!"

"It's not that," said EJ, "where are the beds?"

"You're holding one!" chuckled Sam.

EJ looked down at the blanket draped over his arm.

The foghorn sounded again and EJ heard clanking as the anchor was raised. The *Empire Windrush* was on its way!

17

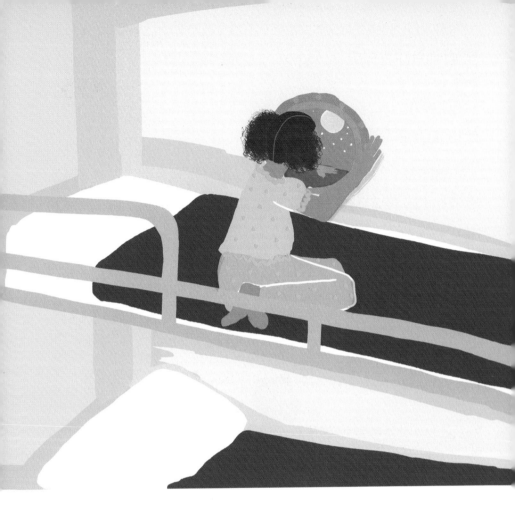

Olivia and Aniyah had settled into their cabin. Olivia was perched on a top bunk, staring at the rising moon from the porthole.

On the bunk next to them, a woman was frantically searching through her things.

"Are you OK?" Aniyah asked.

18

The woman looked at Aniyah. "It's gone!" she cried.

Olivia looked down at them. "What's gone?"

"A family heirloom," the woman said, sadly.

"Heirloom?" Aniyah said. "Like jewellery?"

"Oh no, it's something my husband's father made.
It's a wooden games board … a Ludi board."

The woman sighed. "My husband travelled to Southampton last year. He said I could get plenty of work as a cook, so I'm going to join him in London."

Aniyah looked closely at the woman's face. "Did the Ludi board have paintings of masks on it?" she asked.

"Yes! Have you seen it?" urged the woman.

"Uh no, just a guess. But we can help you look for it. I'm Aniyah and this is Olivia."

The woman smiled. "My name is Maureen Brown."

Aniyah remembered the photographs on the wall of her family restaurant. There was no mistaking it. She'd never met her, but Maureen was Aniyah and EJ's great grandma!

Chapter 4

The next morning, Aniyah couldn't wait to tell EJ about their discovery. She and Olivia ran to the dining area and spotted him eating breakfast.

"It's not fair – you both ended up in a cabin with bunkbeds!" he grumbled.

"That's not important!" Aniyah said. "Great-grandma Maureen came on the *Empire Windrush* to join Great-grandpa in London."

"And?" EJ shoved a bread roll in his mouth.

"We met her!" Aniyah almost shouted.

EJ choked on the bread, and Olivia thumped him on the back.

Aniyah told EJ what Maureen had said.

"It must be the Ludi board we use at the restaurant. We've got to find it!"

They were interrupted by a young man.

"We have some extra bread today. Would you like some –"

"Yes please!" said EJ before he could finish.

"I'm George McPherson. I'm a passenger too but I got a job in the bakery. Anytime you're hungry, let me know and I'll find some food!"

"Are you good at finding other things?" Olivia asked.
"A passenger's lost a large wooden games board."

George thought for a moment. "Mmm, someone left some luggage on the dock. I think it got loaded in the hold. If it's your games board, I'm sure it'll turn up."

Once George had gone, EJ, Aniyah and Olivia made plans.

"I really want to meet Great-grandma, but let's see if we can find the Ludi board first," said EJ.

Aniyah nodded. "We need to look in the hold, find the board and give it to Great-grandma or it may not be there in our time."

HMT EMPIRE WINDRUSH

The ship growled as it pushed through the sea.
Smoke billowed out of the funnels, and passengers, feeling
sick from the motion of the ship, slumped over the top
deck rail.

Olivia, Aniyah and EJ ran past a group of men playing
dominoes on a makeshift table.

"Sam said we'll be onboard for a few weeks," said EJ, as they raced down the stairs from deck to deck.

"This might take a few weeks!" replied Aniyah.

Once they entered the hold, they began to search around the barrels and crates.

"The ship is on the way to Mexico, then Cuba!" said EJ.

"How do you know?" asked Olivia. "Don't tell us, Sam said!" she sighed.

Olivia stood on a creaky plank and brushed cobwebs out of her hair. "This place is creepy! EJ, could you help me with this barrel?"

Aniyah was hoisting a suitcase onto a crate when she heard Olivia gasp. She raced towards Olivia and EJ.

They had found two stowaways!

Chapter 5

"We didn't mean to frighten you," said the man as they shuffled into view.

"We snuck onto the ship –" the woman began.

"Evelyn, we have to be careful," murmured the man.

"It's OK, we won't tell anyone," EJ reassured them, before whispering to Aniyah and Olivia, "Sam said there are 1027 passengers onboard. I guess he was wrong!"

"We're looking for a wooden games board and we were told it might be down here." Olivia described it to them.

"It was over there," said Evelyn, pointing. "Robert heard some men say it was left on the dock by a passenger."

The children looked where she was pointing but there was nothing there.

"Oh yes," said Robert, "but a gentleman came and took it. He was wearing a trilby hat."

Almost all the men onboard wore trilby hats.
It looked like the trail had gone cold.

"I prefer it out here!" Olivia said, when they stomped back up the five decks to the main deck. She shivered as she remembered the cobwebs.

They could hear music, dancing and singing and went to see what was going on.

"Look," said EJ, "it's Sam."

Sam was leaning against the rail, listening. "That's Mona Baptiste and Lord Kitchener," he told them. "He's always making up songs on the spot."

"I've heard of them – Nan plays their music all the time," Aniyah whispered to the others.

"How will we find the Ludi board now?" Olivia asked.

"We'll just have to search every deck. We'll start from the bottom and work our way up," EJ replied.

Every morning, they searched the decks and took food to the stowaways. Every afternoon, they listened to music. But there was no sign of the board.

One day, one of the men playing dominoes at the table on the top deck spoke about some messages he had overheard from the radio room, and people gathered to listen.

"It was a message from England! They were talking about us. It sounds like we're not welcome in the mother country."

"Why did we board this ship?" someone muttered.

"I'm sure it'll work out," said Sam.

"Mum and Aunty Pam said Great-grandma was an amazing cook. Why don't we help her prepare a big feast to cheer everyone up?" Aniyah suggested.

"That's a great idea. As long as EJ's nowhere near the flour!" laughed Olivia.

"It would be nice to spend time with Great-grandma, even though we can't find the Ludi board," EJ said.

He went to find George in the bakery, to see if he could help, while Aniyah and Olivia found Maureen. She looked a little lonely, but she smiled when she saw the girls and listened to their idea.

"I love to cook! We'll need to find some seasoning."

"We'll ask the other passengers for herbs and spices," Aniyah said.

They collected curry, pimento, onion powder, creamed coconut, bags of thyme and tins of ackee and dried peas.

"This is going to be the best feast, ever!" Olivia said.

A few days later, George said the cooks were finished for the day and led them to the kitchen. Maureen showed everyone what to do.

EJ cut the onions, Olivia peeled potatoes and Aniyah kneaded dough.

"You're good at this!" Maureen smiled.

They made hard dough bread, patties, fried fish, curry chicken, rice and peas, and soups with potatoes and dumplings. A delicious smell wafted around the ship.

As darkness fell, the feast began. There was lots of singing and dancing.

"Check this out!" EJ said and swung his arms and legs.

Aniyah looked at Olivia. "Let's show him some real dance moves!"

EJ did a spin and fell headfirst into the men playing dominoes.

"Look!" Olivia pointed to the floor beside EJ. The board the men had been using had turned over. It was Great-grandma's Ludi board!

One of the men explained they'd needed a makeshift table and found the board in the hold.

"I'm sure you can find another one!" Sam said.

Maureen was overjoyed when the children returned the Ludi board to her.

"You have no idea how much this means to me," she said.

Chapter 6

There was a cold breeze when the *Empire Windrush* finally anchored in the River Thames off Tilbury docks and slid alongside the landing stage. After four weeks and one day at sea, the passengers could finally disembark and meet loved ones waiting for them.

EJ and Aniyah's great grandma gave the children a hug. "It was nice to meet you. If you're ever in Hackney, be sure to look me up!"

George grinned and waved goodbye. Sam gave them a salute.

Lord Kitchener was speaking to some of the reporters, who were waiting on the quayside, and he burst into song, *"London is the place for me!"*

Aniyah and EJ hung over the rail and watched their great-grandma, Sam and George walk down the gangplank. They even saw Evelyn and Robert melt into the crowd.

"I'm glad they made it here," said Olivia.

Just then the boat seemed to shake, and bursts of light flashed before their eyes. The wormhole appeared and sucked Aniyah, Olivia and EJ in.

Aunty Pam was still gossiping in the kitchen when the children arrived back at the restaurant. They had been onboard the *Empire Windrush* for almost a month, but it was as if they'd never left.

Aniyah and EJ stared at the Ludi board. Now they knew how precious it was to their great-grandma, they would treasure it even more.

"It's my go," said Olivia. "Let's play!"

Lost and found

REAL PEOPLE

Samuel King MBE
1926–2016

Joined the Royal Air Force in 1944 and fought in the Second World War

Mona Baptiste
1928–1993

Internationally successful singer and actor

Lord Kitchener
1922–2000

Stage name for Aldwyn Roberts, the Grand Master of Calypso

George McPherson

George worked in the bakery and discovered stowaways on board 47

:: Ideas for reading ::

Written by Gill Matthews
Primary Literacy Consultant

Reading objectives:

- check that the text makes sense to them, discuss their understanding and explaining the meaning of words in context
- ask questions to improve their understanding of a text
- draw inferences such as inferring characters' feelings, thoughts and motives from their actions, and justifying inferences with evidence

Spoken language objectives:

- use relevant strategies to build their vocabulary
- articulate and justify answers, arguments and opinions
- participate in discussions, presentations, performances, role play, improvisations and debates

Curriculum links: History: a study of an aspect or theme in British history that extends pupils' chronological knowledge beyond 1066

Interest words: explained, replied, chuckled, cried, urged

Resources: IT

Build a context for reading

- Show children the front cover of the book. Discuss what they can see in the image and what the title means to them.
- Read the back-cover blurb. Explore children's existing knowledge of the *Empire Windrush*.
- Ask what kind of book this is and what they think they are going to read about.

Understand and apply reading strategies

- Read pp2–5 aloud using appropriate expression. Ask where and when the children think the story is taking place. What do they think happens at the end of the chapter? Establish which characters they have met in this chapter.
- Ask children to read pp6–13. Ask where and when they think the children are in this chapter, encouraging them to refer to the text to support their responses. Explore how they think the people on the boat might feel about travelling to the United Kingdom.